The Essential
Seducer

Edited by
PETER HAINING

ROBERT HALE · LONDON

Preface and selection © Peter Haining 1994
First published in Great Britain 1994

ISBN 0 7090 5374 6

Robert Hale Limited
Clerkenwell House
Clerkenwell Green
London EC1R 0HT

The right of Peter Haining to be identified as
author of this work has been asserted by him
in accordance with the Copyright, Designs and
Patents Act 1988.

2   4   6   8   10   9   7   5   3   1

Photoset in North Wales by
Derek Doyle & Associates, Mold, Clwyd.
Printed in Hong Kong by
Bookbuilders Limited

Preface

Seduction has been a part of life on this earth ever since the first man and woman gazed at each other. Indeed, didn't Eve tempt her man, Adam, with the 'Forbidden Fruit' of sex – and haven't their progeny been irresistibly drawn to this same beguiling and dangerous fruit ever since?

Not surprisingly, the oral and written tradition about seduction – the art of 'inducing a person to have sexual intercourse' to quote my copy of *Chambers Dictionary* – dates back to the very earliest period of our history. At about the time of the birth of Christ, for instance, both the Greeks and the Romans had turned it into a highly skilled art form. One of the leading poets of that era, the Latin scholar Ovid, had even written what amounted to the first guidebook to seduction, *Ars Amatoria* (The Art of Love), a volume of instruction and advice that has remained probably unsurpassed by any other work throughout all the subsequent ages of literature.

True, a great many men and women of letters have followed Ovid's example and composed similar guides, as well as novels, stories and poems about seduction, all of which have revealed a profound understanding of human emotions – not to mention a great deal of practical experience! – where this endlessly fascinating subject is concerned. Indeed, in this context I am always reminded of those famous lines by Will Shakespeare, himself no novice in the art:

Oh, what a tangled web we weave,
When first we practise to deceive.

At its most basic, seduction is, of course, a ritual of persuasion by one person who initially wants sex more than the other. This person, however, need no more be a man than a woman – although traditionally the male has most frequently been portrayed as the aggressor, lusting after an objective that has been perhaps most accurately described as 'somewhere between courtship and rape'. But, as my research for this book has proved to me, this is not the whole truth. For there have also been a large number of women and girls who, as a result of curiosity, vanity, frustration or even an unashamed search for pleasure, have been the initiators of sex, too.

Because of this undeniable fact, I have tried in the pages which follow to represent the feelings of both· parties as they have explored the mysteries of this erotic power game and discovered its pleasures and pains, rewards and penalties. *The Essential Seducer* is, I hope, a distillation of experience, experimentation and exhilaration gathered from twenty centuries of devoted practice. It represents the art of the tempter and the tempted in which each new day, each new encounter, promises new opportunities. Is it your turn, dear reader, to be next?

Peter Haining

Acknowledgements

Thanks are due to the following for permission to include copyright material: Faber for the extracts from *On The Edge* by Walter de la Mare and *The Perfect Mistress* by Ronald Duncan; Doubleday & Company for two extracts from *Wit and Wisdom* by H. Allen Smith and an extract from *The Girls of Boston* by George Thompson; A.P. Watt Literary Agency for the extracts from *Letter From Paris* by Dodie Smith and *Cantleman's Spring-Mate* by Wyndham Lewis; Reed Publishing Group for the extract from *Fear of Flying* by Erica Jong, the lines from *Youth* by John Whitworth and the extract from *Rates of Exchange* by Malcolm Bradbury; Penguin Books for the extract from *Love Among The Artists* by George Bernard Shaw; Random Publishing Group for the extracts from *Room at the Top* by John Braine, *On Lady Poltagrue, a Public Peril* by Hilaire Belloc and from *Nothing To Fear* by Kingsley Amis. Acknowledgement is also made to *The Times, Daily Mail, Sunday Times* and the *Independent on Sunday* for extracts from interviews published in their pages. Every effort has been made to seek permission for copyright material in this book, and any omissions from this acknowledgements section will be remedied in any forthcoming edition.

It has been said that any man can have any woman.

WILLIAM HAZLITT (1778-1830)
Liber Amoris

All women can be caught; spread but your nets and you will catch them.

OVID (43BC–AD 18)
Ars Amatoria

Adultery is my nature.

CYRIL TOURNEUR (?1575–1626)
The Revenger's Tragedy

Variety is the spice of love.

ANONYMOUS

Mean I to try, what rash untri'd I sought.
JOHN MILTON (1608–74)
Paradise Lost

Young I am, and yet unskilled
How to make a lover yield,
How to keep, or how to gain,
When to love and when to feign.
ANONYMOUS
Love Triumphant

I long to get a Learned Maidenhead,
Or if Untaught and Ignorant she be,
She takes me then with her Simplicity.
AMORES (1790)

He is a fool who thinks by force or skill
To turn the course of a woman's will.
HENRY SCOTT TUKE (1846–1928)
Poems

There is not so impudent a thing in nature as
the saucy look of an assured man confident of
success.
WILLIAM CONGREVE (1670–1729)
The Way of the World

I won't say I'm Yours,
By day or night, or any kind of light;
Because you are too imprudent.
HARRIETTE WILSON (1786–1846)
Memoirs

Curiosity is an early and dangerous enemy to virtue.
ANONYMOUS

Man has his will, but woman her way.
OLIVER WENDELL HOLMES (1809–94)
The Autocrat of the Breakfast-Table

Every sin is the result of a collaboration.
STEPHEN CRANE (1871–1900)
Wounds in the Rain

When we resist temptation, it is usually because temptation is weak, not because we are strong.
DUC DE LA ROCHEFOUCAULD (1613–80)

And now I give my sensual race the rein:
Fit thy consent to my sharp appetite;
Lay by all nicety and prolixious blushes.
WILLIAM SHAKESPEARE (1564–1616)
Measure for Measure

Men wish to be saved from the mischiefs of their vices, but not from their vices.
RALPH WALDO EMERSON (1803–1882)
Essays

One is always a woman's first lover.
NINON DE LENCLOS (1620–1705)
Memoires

What men call gallantry, and gods adultery,
Is much more common where the climate's sultry.
LORD BYRON (1788–1824)
Don Juan

Being such as nature and habit had made me, could I contemplate so seductive a creature for a great part of the day without being crazy about her?
GIACOMO CASANOVA (1725–98)
Mémoires

One reason why she seduces casual attention is that she never courts it.
THOMAS HARDY (1840–1928)
Tess of the D'Urbervilles

Neither walls, nor goods, nor anything is more difficult to be guarded than woman.
WILLIBALD ALEXIS

A man's sense of honour is so peculiar that it gets out of working condition the minute he gets near a pretty woman.
ANONYMOUS

To bring this business to a happy end you must set a 'love snare'. This expression implies much that is difficult and is, indeed, what is more

commonly known as wife-stealing. Before a man can set about this wife-stealing business with any prospects of success, five things are essential. He must be as handsome as P'an An. His member must be at least as large as a donkey's. He must be rich as Teng T'ung, and reasonably young. Finally, he must have plenty of time on his hands, and almost endless patience. If you are possessed of all these qualifications, you may think of going in for this sort of entertainment.

WANG SHIH-CHÊN (1634–1711)
Chin Ping Mei

Was ever woman in this humour woo'd?
Was ever woman in this humour won?
I'll have her; but I will not keep her long.
WILLIAM SHAKESPEARE (1564–1616)
Richard III

Would she could make of me a saint,
Or I of her a sinner.
WILLIAM CONGREVE (1670–1729)
Pious Selinda Goes to Prayers

'Tis no sin love's fruits to steal,
But the sweet thefts to reveal:
To be taken, to be seen,
These have crimes accounted been.
BEN JONSON (1572/3–1637)
Volpone

I must make love to you, pretty Miss. Will you let me make love to you?
WILLIAM CONGREVE (1670–1729)
Love for Love

He was al coltish, ful of passion,
And ful of jargon as a flekked [mag]pie.
GEOFFREY CHAUCERY (*c.* 1343–1400)
The Canterbury Tales

It was Clara whom he meant to seduce. Her seduction was quite determined upon … He had very early seen the necessity of the case, and had now been long trying with cautious assiduity to make an impression on her heart and to undermine her principles.
JANE AUSTEN (1775–1817)
Sanditon

A rascal far gone in lechery
Lured maids to their doom by his treachery.
He invited them in
For the purpose of sin,
Though he said 'twas to look at his etchery.
ANONYMOUS

It is the ladies who first created cuckoldry and they who put the horns on their husband's heads.
ABBÉ DE BRANTOME (*c.* 1534–1614)
Vies des Dames Galantes

Many a good husband hasn't the nerve or the courage to be anything else.
HENRY ROWLAND (1871–1936)
Miscellany

The tempter or the tempted – who sins most?
ANONYMOUS

To speak of love is to make love.
HONORÉ DE BALZAC (1799–1850)
Physiologie du Marriage

When all is done I find that love is nothing else but an insatiate thirst of enjoying greedily a desired subject. Nor Venus that good huswife, other than a tickling delight of emptying one's seminary vessels: as is the pleasure which nature giveth us to discharge other parts, which becommeth faulty by immoderation and defective by indiscretion.

    MICHEL MONTAIGNE (1533–92)
    Essais

There is room for delicate artifice in love-making, and a skilled but low cunning, other than Nature's, in lust-inciting.

    WALTER DE LA MARE (1873–1956)
    On the Edge

Men were born to lie and women to believe them.

JOHN GAY (1685–1732)
Trivia

A man marries a woman because she appeals to his 'higher nature' – and then spends the rest of his life seeking after those who appeal to his lower nature.

HENRY ROWLAND (1871–1936)
Miscellany

The measure of a man's real character is what he would do if he knew he would never be found out.

THOMAS MACAULAY (1800–59)
Trivia

The only original thing about some men is original sin.

ANONYMOUS

Man argues woman may not be trusted too far; woman feels man cannot be trusted too near.

CHARLES FARRAR BROWNE (1834–67)
Artemus Ward, His Book

Sir Edward's great objective was to be seductive. With such personal advantages as he knew himself to possess, and such talents as he did also give himself credit for, he regarded it as his duty. He felt that he was formed to be a dangerous man.

JANE AUSTEN (1775–1817)
Sanditon

The place to carry on an affair with the daughter is behind her father's back. It is the lover's business to make her willing to see father and mother in Hell rather than lose him.
JOHANN SCHILLER (1759–1805)
Die Horen

A girl of sixteen accepts love; a woman of thirty incites it.
JOSEPH RICARD

Young men want to be faithful and are not; old men want to be faithless and cannot.
OSCAR WILDE (1854–1900)
Complete Works

Too easy a success in love deprives it of its charm; hindrances add to its value.
STENDHAL (1783–1842)
Le Rouge et le Noir

And now she lets him whisper in her ear,
Flatter, entreat, promise, protest and swear,
Yet ever as he greedily assay'd
To touch those dainties, she the harpy play'd,
And every limb did as a soldier stout
Defend the fort, and keep the foeman out.
    CHRISTOPHER MARLOWE (1564–93)
    Hero and Leander

I would not have you fettered to one lady –
Impossible – even to a bride!
Provided, of course, the itch is satisfed with
    discretion.
    OVID (43 BC–AD 18)
    Ars Amatoria

Every man requireth at least two soulmates.
One to amuse him, and one to wait upon him.
    ANONYMOUS

If either should form a temporary attachment outside the bonds of matrimony it will be a trifling affair that will not alter or spoil in the slightest degree their mutual understanding.
BRITISH SOCIAL HYGIENE COUNCIL (1936)
Preparation For Marriage

For wanton women lascivious men are made; in like manner lascivious men for wanton women.
MOUAMMED (*c.* 570–632)

Of all sexual aberrations perhaps the most peculiar is chastity.
REMY de GOURMONT (1858–1915)
Promenades Philosophiques

Give me chastity and continency – but not yet!
ST AUGUSTINE (AD 354-430)
Confessions, book viii, chapter 7

The greatest of all sins is the sin of love-making; it is so great that it takes two persons to commit it.
CARDINAL CAMUS (1740–1804)
Works

Carnal desire enflaming, he on Eve
Began to cast lascivious Eyes, she him
As wantonly repaid; in Lust they burne:
Till Adam thus 'gan Eve to dalliance move.
JOHN MILTON (1608–74)
Paradise Lost

Eve was the first woman who fooled her man.
JOSH BILLINGS (1818–85)
Billing's Almanac

Rely not on women, trust not to their hearts,
Whose joys and whose sorrows are hung to
        their parts!
Lying love they will swear thee when guile
        ne'er departs
Eve ousted Adam – see ye not? – through
        their arts.
    THE ARABIAN NIGHTS
    Translated by Sir Richard Burton
        (1821–90)

Most women spend their lives in robbing the old
tree from which Eve plucked the first fruit.
    OCTAVE FEUILLET (1821–1890)
    Scènes et Proverbes

To hear her whisper women's lore so well,
And every word she spoke entic'd him on.
    JOHN KEATS (1795–1821)
    Lamia

Opposition is the very spur of love.
    TOBIAS SMOLLETT (1721–71)
    Peregrine Pickle

Women have the same desires as men, but do
not have the same right to express them.
    JEAN-JACQUES ROUSSEAU (1712–78)
    Confessions

There are different kinds of love, but they have
all the same aim: possession.
    ANONYMOUS

Seduction is a circulating library in which we
seldom ask twice for the same volume.
    NATHANIEL PARKER WILLIS (1806–1867)
    Pencillings by the Way

She looks like the de luxe edition of a wicked French novel meant especially for the English market.

    OSCAR WILDE (1854–1900)
    Complete Works

Some take a lover, some take drams or prayers,
Some mind their household, others dissipation,
From the dull palace to the dirty hovel:
Some play the devil, and then write a novel.

    LORD BYRON (1788–1824)
    Don Juan

Are women books? Would mine were an Almanack, to change her every year.

    BENJAMIN FRANKLIN (1706–90)
    Poor Richard's Almanac

The man who gets on best with women is the one who knows best how to get on without them.

    CHARLES BAUDELAIRE (1821–67)
    Petits Poèmes en Prose

Bianca: My lord, what seek you?
Duke of Florence: Love
Bianca: 'Tis gone already;
I have a husband.
Duke: That's a single comfort;
Take a friend to him.

    THOMAS MIDDLETON (1580–1627)
    Women Beware Women

I hate a woman who seems to be hermetically sealed in the lower regions.
     H. ALLEN SMITH (1864–1959)
     Wit and Wisdom

Do not be weary of praising her looks, her hair, her shapely fingers, her small foot: even honest girls love to hear their charms extolled; even to the chaste their beauty is a care and a delight.
     OVID (43 BC–AD 18)
     Ars Amatoria

The only way to behave to a woman is to make love to her if she is pretty and to someone else if she is plain.
     OSCAR WILDE (1854–1900)
     Complete Works

There was no wisdom in it – to bid an artist, an old seducer, to a female banquet.
     JOHN FLETCHER (1579–1625)
     Rule of a Wife

To RUIN a woman, to rob her of her honour, or (what is worse to many of them) of the reputation of it. Terrible as this word sounds, there are of them, who would look on no unhappiness so great as that of having no reason *ever* to fear it would be attempted. 'Do you want to ruin me?' is a phrase of capitulation: a kind of dying-speech of virtue, just going to be turned off.

THE DICTIONARY OF LOVE (1924)

There are two things a real man likes – danger and play; and he likes women because they are the most dangerous of playthings.

FREDIERICH NIETZSCHE (1844–1900)
Genealogie der Moral

Love finds an altar for forbidden fires.

ALEXANDER POPE (1688–1744)
Essay on Man

All things in the world are expended by usage –
except lust which is augmented by practice.
ABBÉ DE BRANTOME (*c*.1534–1614)
Vies des Dames Galantes

When I'm good, I'm very good – but when I'm
bad I'm better.
MAE WEST (1892–1984)
Goodness Had Nothing To Do With It

Professional seducers are not ignorant of the
inevitable boredom of marriage. They abstain
from assailing young wives before the lapse of
several months of married life. They await with
patience their forthcoming reward, knowing
well that in marriage itself, in conjugal
familiarity, there takes place a kind of training,
of preparation for their projects. When conjugal
life is finally established the wife soon feels she
misses the delicious torment, this trouble which
now belongs to the past. A longing for the past
with the virtuous woman, desire for adventure
in the others; how many feel the need of a new
liaison in which all that was exquisite in the
first initiation begins again!
MARCEL PREVOST (1697–1763)
The Secret Garden

He that would woo a maid must feign, lie and
flatter;
But he that woos a widow must down with
his britches and at her.
DODIE SMITH (1901–1979)
Letter from Paris

A man who is known to have broken many hearts is naturally invested with a tantalising charm to women who have hearts yet to be broken.

DAVID BOYESEN

The most ordinary and respectable of men will, when with others, try to appear the rake with women.

HONORÉ DE BALZAC (1799–1850)
Comédie Humaine

Wouldn't it be nice to be like men and just get notches in your belt and sleep with the most attractive men and not get emotionally involved?

MARILYN MONROE (1926–1962)

The reason that a woman who takes the downward path has so much attention is that there are so many men going that way.

HENRY ROWLAND (1871–1936)
Miscellany

One ought never to allow them time to think,
their vivacity being prodigious and their
foresight exceedingly short and limited. The
first hurry of their passions, if they are but
vigorously followed, is what is generally most
favourable to lovers.
ANONYMOUS

He began with that happy snare to all women,
viz, taking notice upon all occasions how pretty
I was, as he called it, how agreeable, how
well-carriaged, and the like; and this he
contrived so subtly, as if he had known as well
how to catch a woman in his net as a partridge
when he went a setting.
DANIEL DEFOE (1660–1731)
Moll Flanders

Woman is an overgrown child that one amuses
with toys, intoxicates with flattery and seduces
with promises.
MATTHEW ARNOLD (1822–88)
Mixed Essays

It is easier for a woman to defend her virtue
against men than her reputation against
women.
JEAN ROCHEBRUNE

Uncertain as the sea is woman's nature.
ANONYMOUS

I marvel why the chaster of your sex
Should think this pretty toy called
    maidenhead

31

So strange a loss; when, being lost, 'tis
   nothing,
And you are still the same.
    JOHN FORD (1586–after 1639)
    'Tis Pity She's A Whore

The ability to make love frivolously is the chief
characteristic which distinguishes human
beings from the beasts.
    HEYWOOD BROUN (1888–1939)
    It Seems to Me

Lovers themselves will follow their passion
And imitate this new French passion;
And with false heart and member too,
Rich widows for convenience woo.
    ANONYMOUS

It's easier to hide your light under a bushel
than to keep your shady side dark.
    ANONYMOUS

If you talk a word more of your honour, you'll
make me incapable to wrong it. To talk of
honour in the mysteries of love is like talking of
Heaven or the Deity in an operation of
witchcraft just when you are employing the
devil – it makes the charm impotent.
    WILLIAM WYCHERLEY (1641–1715)
    The Country Wife

She wore far too much rouge last night and not
quite enough clothes; that is always a sign of
desire in a woman.
    OSCAR WILDE (1854–1900)
    Complete Works

Woman is a pill and must be gilded when she is taken.

ANONYMOUS

I am soon undone
And as soon done.

FRANCIS BEAUMONT (1584–1616) and JOHN
FLETCHER 1579–1625)
The Maid's Tragedy

A man unbuttons a woman's dress with almost the same grace and alacrity that a woman displays in climbing a barbed wire fence.

HENRY ROWLAND (1871–1936)
Miscellany

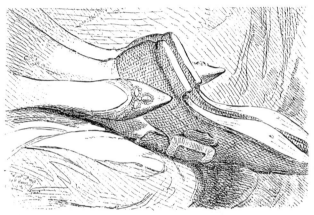

She was charmingly dressed, and soon aroused desires in him that he longed to gratify, if he could get the opportunity. She was alone, which was an obstacle less in the way.

THE LASCIVIOUS HYPOCRITE (1824)

A sweet disorder in the dress
Kindles in clothes a wantonness:
A winning wave (deserving note)
In the tempestuous petticoat:
A careless shoestring, in whose tie
I see a wild civility:
Do more bewitch me, than when art
Is too precise in every part.

ROBERT HERRICK (1591–1674)
Delight in Disorder

The modesty which appears so deeply rooted in women's hearts really goes no further than the clothes they wear and when they are plucked off no trace of it remains.

CLEMENT OF ALEXANDRIA (b. *c.* AD 160)
Miscellanies

Dress to meet your parents; undress to meet your lover.

CHINESE PROVERB

Happy the man who in his pocket keeps,
Whether with green or scarlet ribbon bound,
A well-made cundum – he, nor dreads the ills
Of cankers, gonorrhoeas or poxes dire.

ANONYMOUS
A Panegyrick Upon Cundums

Dildoes, without the least disgrace,
May well supply the lover's place,
And make our girls ne'er care for 't,
Though 'twere their fortune to go bare-foot.

SAMUEL BUTLER (1613–80)
Dildoes

I'd have you, quoth he.
Would you have me? quoth she;
O where, sir?
In my chamber, quoth he.
In your chamber? quoth she;
Why there, sir?
To kiss you, quoth he.
To kiss me? quoth she;
O why, sir?
'Cause I love it, quoth he.
Do you love it? quoth she;
So do I, sir.
THE WINDSOR DROLLERY (1819)

Were it not for imagination, a man would be as happy in the arms of a chambermaid as of a duchess.
SAMUEL JOHNSON (1709–84)
James Boswell, *Life of Johnson*

I read of a man in the paper
Whose daughter took up the theatre
A scoundrel easily seduced her.
    WILHELM BUSCH (1832–1908)
    Critique of the Heart

A girl, standing alone, will seldom allow herself to be seduced, because she lacks the courage. But if she has a companion, she yields easily; of course, in such cases the man needs a double portion of cunning but he will also find a rich reward for his trouble. That's why I can assure all parents who allow their daughter to take a walk with a young man without any scruple, that the moment a girl friend accompanies them their darling is lost, provided the young man understands his business.
    GIACOMO CASANOVA (1725–98)
    Mémoires

Who that has seen a woman wavering lie
Betwixt her shame and curiosity,
Knowing her sex's failing, will not deem,
That in the balance shame would kick the
beam?
    LORD BYRON (1788–1824)
    Don Juan

My woman says she'll never be the lover of any man, or even Jove himself. She says so. What a woman says to an eager lover, write in the water, write in the rushing waves.
    CATULLUS (*c.*84–*c.*54 BC)
    To a Mistress

A man assumes that a woman's refusal is just part of the game. Or, at any rate, a lot of men assume that. When a man says no, it's no. When a woman says no, it's yes, or at least maybe.

ERICA JONG (1942–)
Fear of Flying

That crafty girl shall please me best,
That No for Yea can say;
And every wanton, willing kiss
Can season with a Nay.

THOMAS HEYWOOD (?1574–1641)
Love's Maistresse

Between the yes and no of a woman I would not undertake to thrust the point of a pin.

ANONYMOUS

Women resist in order to be conquered.

OTTAVIO PICCOLOMINI (1599–1656)
Essays

Now in his vigorous grasp, half-won she
    pants,
Struggles, denies – yet in denying, grants!
ANONYMOUS

A lisping young lady named Beth
Was saved from a fate worse than death
    Seven times in a row,
    Which unsettled her so,
That she quit saying 'No' and said, 'Yeth'.
ANONYMOUS

The resistance of a woman is not always proof
of her virtue, but more frequently of her
experience.
NINON DE LENCLOS (1620–1705)
Memoires

Maids' nays are nothing, they are shy
But do desire what they deny.
ROBERT HERRICK (1591–1674)
Hesperides

A woman begins by resisting a man's advances
and ends by blocking his retreat.
OSCAR WILDE (1854–1900)
Complete Works

I wish all maids be warned by me,
Never to trust man's courtesy;
For if we do but chance to bow,
They'll use us then they care not how.
ANONYMOUS

Vanity ruins more women than love.
MME MARIE DEFFAND (1697–1780)

A man seldom escapes temptation because he is
so careful not to let any interesting temptations
escape him.
HENRY ROWLAND (1871–1936)
Miscellany

Appetite is the very essence of man … between
appetite and desire there is no difference save
that desire is self-conscious appetite.
BARUCH SPINOZA (1632–77)
Ethica

Farewell to that maid who will be undone
Who in markets of men (where plenty
Are cried up and down) will die even for one;
I will live to make fools of twenty.
    SIR WILLIAM D'AVENANT (1606–68)
    The Unfortunate Lovers

Pleasure's a sin, and sometimes sin's a pleasure.
    LORD BYRON (1788–1824)
    Don Juan

Wicked women bother one; good women bore one; that is the only difference between them.
    OSCAR WILDE (1854–1900)
    Complete Works

'But' she said, 'real liking does not grow as quickly as a view of a body and legs.'
    'Pardon me,' I rejoined, 'but passion, desire in

a man comes first: it's for the woman to transform it into enduring affection.'
FRANK HARRIS (1856–1931)
My Life and Loves

Every woman is infallibly to be gained by every sort of flattery and every man by one sort or another.
THE FOURTH EARL OF CHESTERFIELD (1694–1773)
Letters

One kiss cannot bestow the sweetness of a thousand, but may bestow more assurance than a million.
RICHARD GARNETT (1789–1850)
De Flagello Myrteo

He admired the elevation of her soul and the lace of her petticoat.
GUSTAVE FLAUBERT (1821–80)
Madame Bovary

Peace is his aim, his gentleness is such,
And he loves love, for he loves screwing much.
Nor are his high desires above his strength:
His sceptre and his tool are of a length,
And she may sway the one who plays with t'other.
JOHN WILMOT, SECOND EARL OF ROCHESTER (1647–80)
A Satire on Charles II

Charlot took the copy of Ovid and placed herself by the Duke who opened it just at the love of Myrra for her father. His eyes feasted themselves upon her face, thence wandered over her snowy bosom, and saw the young swelling breasts just beginning to distinguish themselves and which were gently heaving at the impressions of Myrra's sufferings. By this dangerous reading he pretended to show her that there were pleasures her sex were born for and which she might consequently long to taste!

MARY DELARIVIÈRE MANLEY (1663–1724)
The New Atalantis

There was a young student named Jones,
Who'd reduce any maiden to moans
    By his wonderful knowledge,
    Acquired in college,
Of nineteen erogenous zones.

ANONYMOUS

A man's conscience is made of India rubber – warranted to stretch as long as the fun lasts.

HENRY ROWLAND (1871–1936)
Miscellany

Rather than anyone shall prejudice your honour, madam, I'll prejudice theirs. To serve you, I'll lie with them all, make the secret their own, and then they'll keep it. I am a Machiavel in love, madam.

WILLIAM WYCHERLEY (1641–1715)
The Country Wife

Women rather take to terrible people. Prize
fighters, pirates, highwaymen, rebel generals,
randy Turks and Bluebeards generally have a
fascination for the sex; your virgin has a
natural instinct to saddle your lion.

OLIVER WENDELL HOLMES (1809–94)
The Autocrat of the Breakfast-Table

Bluebeard isn't the only bridegroom who ever
went to the altar with a closet full of dead loves
on his conscience.

HENRY ROWLAND (1871–1936)
Miscellany

With the gesture of a fabulous Faust he drew
her against him, and kissed her with a crafty
gentleness.

WYNDHAM LEWIS (1882–1957)
Cantleman's Spring-Mate

Age cannot wither her, nor custom stale
Her infinite variety. Other women cloy
The appetites they feed; but she makes
hungry
Where she most satisfies.
    WILLIAM SHAKESPEARE (1564–1616)
    Antony and Cleopatra

The first day I saw Richard Burton he sort of
sidled over to me and said, 'Has anyone ever
told you that you're a very pretty girl?' And I
said to myself, '*Oy gevaldt*, here's the great
lover, the great wit, the great intellectual from

Wales and he comes out with a chat-up line like
that!'
ELIZABETH TAYLOR (1932–)

Maidens, like moths, are ever caught by glare.
LORD BYRON (1788–1824)
Don Juan

Aware of my intentions, she admonished me
that a gentleman would never attempt to
seduce a lady on her wedding day. I replied that
a lady would never put herself in a position
where she was seducable – on either her
wedding day or any other day – unless she
desired to be seduced.
GIACOMO CASANOVA (1725–98)
Mémoires

I treat the charwomen like duchesses, and the
duchesses like charwomen.
BEAU BRUMMELL (1778–1840)
Life of Beau Brummell

I was sorry to hear that Sir W. Pen's maid Betty
was gone away yesterday, for I was in hopes to
have had a bout with her before she had gone,
she being very pretty. I had also a mind to my
own wench, but I dare not for fear she should
prove honest and refuse and then tell my wife.
SAMUEL PEPYS (1633–1703)
The Diary of Samuel Pepys

Men always want to be a woman's first love;
women have a more subtle instinct: what they
like is to be a man's last romance.
OSCAR WILDE (1854–1900)
Complete Works

The thing that takes up the least amount of time and causes the most amount of trouble is sex.

JOHN BARRYMORE (1882–1942)
Confessions of an Actor

Men fancy me because I don't wear a brassiere. And women like me because I don't look like a girl who would steal a husband – at least, not for long.

JEAN HARLOW (1911–1937)

When the lights are out all women are beautiful.

ERROL FLYNN (1909–1959)

It's not the men in my life, it's the life in my men that counts.

MAE WEST (1892–1984)
Goodness Had Nothing To Do With It

I have genuinely fancied quite a few mega-rich women on both sides of the Atlantic and pursued that attraction. The horror part of the story inevitably came when meeting the parents. It is surprising how quickly a doting father can come up with a question about my nickname, 'What exactly does "Seducer of the Valleys" mean?'

DAI LLEWELLYN (1943–)
The Times

The majority of readers will imagine, I dare swear, that his lordship immediately nailed the fair one down upon the couch with kisses, and that his desires and resolutions giving him double vigour, in spite of prayers, tears and strugglings, he forced his way into the seat of bliss. But his lordship was a more experienced engineer than so.

ANONYMOUS
History of the Countess of B

Take great care that the first impressions you give of yourself may be not only favourable, but pleasing, engaging, nay – seducing.

THE FOURTH EARL OF CHESTERFIELD (1694–1773)
Letters

Vary the times of your adultery;
Vary the places where you meet your mistress,
In case a rival knows her secret too.

OVID (43 BC–AD 18)
Ars Amatoria

Women often deceive to conceal what they feel; men to simulate what they do not feel – love.
ERNEST LEGOUVE (1807–1903)
Soixante Ans de Souvenirs

You may strike out, so to speak, a window in the lady's breast through which you can contemplate pretty accurately the composition and working of her mental machinery.
ANONYMOUS
How to Woo and How to Win

He who cannot keep a secret knows not how to love.
STENDHAL (1783–1842)
Le Rouge et le Noir

A man is in no danger so long as he talks his love; but to write it is to impale himself on his own pot-hooks.
DOUGLAS JERROLD (1803–57)

Entice her to read, but suffer her not to look into Rabelais or Scarron or Don Quixote – for they are books which exite laughter and thou knowest that there is no passion so serious as lust.
LAURENCE STERNE (1713–68)
Tristram Shandy

Mere idleness has ruined more women than passion, vanity more than idleness, and credulity more than either.
CHARLES CALEB COLTON (1780–1832)
Lacon

Licence my roving hands, and let them go,
Before, behind, between, above, below.
O my America, my new-found-land,
My kingdom, safest when one man man'd.
   JOHN DONNE (1572–1631)
   Sonnet to Pleasure

You must talk prettily to the woman, but you must not be too rough when you begin to take liberties. If you touch her too soon you will spoil the game. But it is possible that you might knock down a pair of chop-sticks with your sleeve and touch her foot when you pretend to pick them up. This may make her angry, but the chances are she will not be and if she says nothing the game is won.
   CLEMENT EGERTON
   The Golden Lotus

If men knew all that women think, they would be twenty times more audacious.

ALPHONSE KARR
Les Guêpes

Soft easy ways thou should not always
    choose,
But sometimes acts of Force and Manhood
    use:
Thy toying Plays, and pretty gamesome
    Wiles,
Are sometimes mixed with more laborious
    Toils.
Of Stratagems of Wit are your best course,
And sometimes you thrive best by down-right
    Force.

ELEGIES OF OLD AGE (*c.* 18th century)

'Tis one great point of love, first to
    impose
Upon our own belief, so self-deceived
Are better fitted to deceive another.
    MARY DELARIVIÈRE MANLEY (1663–1724)
    The Royal Mischief

The eyes start love; intimacy perfects it.
    PUBLILIUS SYRUS, 1st century BC
    Essays

As Chloe o'er the meadows past,
I viewed the lovely maid:
She turned and blushed, renewed her haste,
And feared by me to be embraced:
My eyes my wish betrayed.
    SIR CHARLES SEDLEY (?1639–1701)
    The Fall

A man must be a fool who does not succeed in
making a woman believe that which flatters
her.
    HONORÉ DE BALZAC (1799–1850)
    Contes Drôlatiques

At various local watering holes
I plot the moves of sex like chess
Between each Laura Ashley dress.
    JOHN WHITWORTH (1942–)
    Youth

When ogling a female, Frenchmen start at the
ankles and work their way up. British men
start at the breasts and work their way down.
    PAUL STEINER
    Useless Facts About Women

Asking a girl if you may kiss her before doing it is an insulting way of laying all the responsibility on her.

HENRY ROWLAND (1871–1936)
Miscellany

Various are the hearts of women; use a thousand means to ensnare as many hearts. The same earth bears not everything; this soil suits vines, that olives; in that, wheat thrives. Hearts have as many fashions as the world has shapes; the wise man will suit himself to countless fashions.

OVID (43 BC–AD 18)
Ars Amatoria

Coquetry is the champagne of love.

THOMAS HOOD

If you want to get over a girl never flurry her till her stomach's full of meat and wine; let the food work. Talk a little quiet smut while eating, just to make her laugh and think of bawdy things. That will make her randy.

> WALTER
> *My Secret Life*

Wine gives courage and makes men apt for passion ... At such times often have women bewitched the minds of men, and Venus in the wine has been fire in fire.

> OVID (43 BC–AD 18)
> *Ars Amatoria*

Scandal's the sweetener of a female feast.

> WILLIAM COWPER (1731–1800)
> *The Task*

There was a young lady of Kent
Who said she knew what it meant

When men asked her to dine,
Gave her cocktails and wine;
She knew what it meant, but she went.
ANONYMOUS

Of course men admire a circumspect woman above all things, but they seldom invite her out to supper.
ANONYMOUS

Men used to marry good cooks and seduce chorus girls; now they marry chorus girls and hire good cooks.
THOMAS ROWLAND (1871–1936)
Miscellany

Marriage is not a justifiable plea for the refusal of love.
TWELFTH-CENTURY CODE OF LAWS

I mustn't give the impression that Bratton was anything of a lady-killer or a professional philanderer. Far from it. He was not particularly handsome – dark, prematurely grey – whatever he wore he achieved a shabby appearance. I suppose the quality that women found irresistible in him was that he at first gave them the impression that he did not need them; then, at the last, the belief that he needed no other. He never offered a woman anything but his need.
RONALD DUNCAN (1914–)
The Perfect Mistress

She that denies me, I would have;
Who craves me, I despise.
ANONYMOUS

The fickleness of the women I love is only equalled by the infernal constancy of the women who love me.
GEORGE BERNARD SHAW (1856–1950)
Love Among the Artists

Rascal! That word on the lips of a woman, addressed to a too daring man, often means angel!
ANONYMOUS

The only way to get rid of temptation is to yield to it.
OSCAR WILDE (1854–1900)
Complete Works

He who has taken kisses, if he take not the rest beside, will deserve to lose even what was granted. You may use force. Women like you to

use force. They often wish to give unwillingly what they like to give. She whom a sudden assault has taken by storm is pleased, and counts the audacity as a compliment. But she who, when she might have been compelled, departs untouched, though her looks feign joy, will yet be sad.

> OVID (43 BC–AD 18)
> *Ars Amatoria*

He looked upon the simple bud of beauty at his side, and in spite of the hardness of his heart, shuddered as he thought of his base purpose; the sense of right which had not been completely cast into oblivion by his passions and dissolute course of life, brought before him the extent of the injury he was about to inflict upon her, and almost persuaded him to leave that gem of her sex, her virtue; but the demon of passion whispered in his ears, and right was stifled by the hint that marriage would set all things right, and as he cast his eyes upon her youthful face, he swore, perhaps sincerely, at that time, that she should not suffer by yielding herself to him ...

> GEORGE THOMPSON (1931–)
> *The Girls of Boston*

When a man says he had pleasure with a woman, he does not mean conversation.

> SAMUEL JOHNSON (1709–84)
> *Life of Johnson*

Though a little frightened, she let him have his way, and the reckless, shameless sensuality shook her to her foundations, stripped her to the very last, and made a different woman of her. It was not really love. It was not voluptuousness. It was sensuality sharp and seering as fire, burning the soul to tinder.

D.H. LAWRENCE (1885–1930)
Lady Chatterley's Lover

No, no, for my virginity,
When I lose that, says Rose, I'll die;
Behind the elms, last night, cried Dick,
Rose, were you not extremely sick?

MATTHEW PRIOR (1664–1721)
A True Mind

Come, Madam, come, all rest my powers
    defie,
Until I labour, I in labour lie.

The foe oft-times having the foe in sight,
Is tired with standing though he never fight.
JOHN DONNE (1572–1631)
To His Mistress Going to Bed

Thus I gave up myself to ruin without the least concern, and am a fair memento to all young women whose vanity prevails over their virtue.
DANIEL DEFOE (1660–1731)
Moll Flanders

At length o'ercome she suffers with a sigh
Her ravish'd lover use his victory,
And gave him leave to punish her delay
With double vigour in the am'rous play.
But then, alas! soon ended the delight,
For too much love had hastened its flight,
And every ravish'd sense too soon awake,
Rapt up in bliss it did but now partake:
Which left the lovers in a state to prove
Long were the pains but short the joys of love.
THE BRISTOL DROLLERY (1820)

This time she did not play the frightened virgin; this time I had no scruples, no horizon but the hot lunacy of my own instincts.
JOHN BRAINE (1922–)
Room at the Top

Imagine the girl's surprise when she walked into the playboy's apartment and discovered that he had no chairs, no table, no bed – in fact, no furniture at all.
She was floored!
ANONYMOUS

One night, they say, one single night, makes
tame a woman in a man's arms.

EURIPIDES (480–406 BC)

Bacchae

For a whole night I had a wanton mistress
her lewd inventions were beyond compare.

MARCUS VALERIUS MARTIALIS (*c.* AD 40–104)

Vers de Circonstance

Plato says it is best to think lying down.

ANONYMOUS

A dozen wanton words, put in your head,
Will make you livelier in your lover's bed.

FRANCIS BEAUMONT(1584-1616) and JOHN

FLETCHER (1579–1625)

The Maid's Tragedy

I have chased her fears away
    And instead
    Of Virginhead
Given her a greater good
Perfection and Womanhood.

JOSEPH RUTTER

The Shepherd's Holiday

They got up at last, she went furtively back to
her home; Cantleman on his walk to camp, had
a smile of severe satisfaction on his face. It did
not occur to him that his action might be
supremely unimportant as far as Stella was
concerned. He had not even asked himself if,
had he not been there that night, someone else
might have been there in his place.

WYNDHAM LEWIS (1882–1957)

Cantleman's Spring-Mate

There was a young fellow named Baker,
Who seduced a vivacious young Quaker,
  And when he had done it,
  She straightened her bonnet,
And said: 'I give thanks to my maker.'
ANONYMOUS

While I am making love to a courtesan I do not
fear that the husband may return from the
country, that the door be broken into bits, that
the dog bark, that the house be stirred from top
to bottom, that the woman jump out of bed
quite pale and bewail her being unfortunate,
and that I myself tremble on my own account.
For in such a case you must flee with bare feet
and disordered clothing or beware of your
purse, your buttocks and your reputation.
HORACE (65–8 BC)
Odes

When love begins to count the risk, it's time to
beat a retreat.
DE MADRID

Let it be known that all women of whatever
age, rank, profession or degree, whether virgin,
maid, wife or widow, that shall from and after
this Act impose upon, reduce and betray into
matrimony any of His Majesty's subjects by
means of scents, paints, cosmetics, artificial
teech, false hair, Spanish wool, iron stays,
hoops, high-heeled shoes or bolstered hips and
bosoms, shall incur the penalty the law now in
force against Witchcraft and like misdemean-

ours, and that the marriage upon conviction
shall stand null and void …
ACT OF PARLIAMENT, 1770

Her throat was serpent, but the words she
spake came as through honey.
ANONYMOUS

For that high-born beauty so hemmed him
    about,
Made so plain her meaning, the man must
    needs
Either take her tendered love or distastefully
    refuse.
ANONYMOUS
Sir Gawain and the Green Knight

No sooner had the amorous parley ended, and
the lady had unmasked the royal battery, by
carelessly letting her handkerchief drop from
her neck, than the heart of Mr Jones was

entirely taken, and the fair conqueror enjoyed the usual fruits of her victory.

HENRY FIELDING (1707–54)
Tom Jones

Womankind more joy discovers
Making fools than keeping lovers.

JOHN WILMOT, SECOND EARL OF ROCHESTER
(1647–80)
Sodom

The wisest homely woman can make a man of sense a fool, but the veriest fool of a beauty can make an ass of a statesman.

COLLEY CIBBER (1671–1757)
Melancholy

And her two lilly paps aloft display'd
And all, that might his melting heart entise
To her delights, she unto him betray'd:
The rest hid underneath, him more desirous
    made.

EDMUND SPENSER (*c*.1552–99)
The Faerie Queene

And cunningly to yield herself she
    sought:
Seeming not won, yet won she was at length,
In such wars women use but half their
    strength.
    CHRISTOPHER MARLOWE (1564–93)
    Hero and Leander

In short, if he had known me, and how easy the
trifle he aimed at was to be had, he would have
troubled his head no further, but have lain with
me the next time he had come at me.
    DANIEL DEFOE (1660–1731)
    Moll Flanders

There was a young lady named Smith
Whose virtue was largely a myth.
    She said, 'Try as I can
    I can't find a man
Who it's fun to be virtuous with.'
    ANONYMOUS

Coquette – a female general who builds her
fame on her advances.
    EUGENE FIELD (1850–95)
    A Little Book of Western Verse

Oh! since we last conversed together, a dreadful
veil has been rent from before my eyes. I love
you no longer with the devotion which is paid to
a saint; I prize you no more for the virtues of
your soul; I lust for the enjoyment of your
person. The woman reigns in my bosom, and I
am become a prey to the wildest of passions.
Away with friendship! 'tis a cold unfeeling

word: my bosom burns with love, with unutterable love, and love must be its return.
MATTHEW LEWIS (1775–1818)
The Monk

Wiles and deceits are woman's specialities.
AESCHYLUS (525–456 BC)
Suppliants

Once Antigonus was told his son was ill and went to see him. At the door he met a seductive young girl. He sat down on the bed and took his son's pulse.

'The fever,' said the son, 'has just left me.'

'Oh, yes,' replied the father, 'I met it going out at the door.'
PLUTARCH (AD *c*.50–*c*.125)
Plutarch's Lives

A woman may live without a lover, but a lover once admitted, she never goes through life with only one. She is deserted and cannot bear her anguish and solitude, and hence fills up the void with a second idol.
EDWARD BULWER-LYTTON (1803–73)
Eugene Aram

She who for years protracts her lover's pain,
And makes him wish, and wait, and sigh in
    vain,
To be his wife, when late she gives consent,

Finds half his passion was in courtship
    spent;
Whilst they who boldly all delays remove,
Find every hour a fresh supply of love.
    SUSANNAH CENTLIVRE (1669–1723)
    The Wonder

Man is such a paradox that a woman is forced
to make him believe that she doesn't take him
seriously, or she won't get a chance to take him
at all.
    HENRY ROWLAND (1871–1936)
    Miscellany

A woman finds small difference (in respect of the world) between being naughty and being *thought* naughty.

GIOVANNI GUAZZO

It is far easier to find a woman who has not sinned at all than a woman who has sinned but once.

DUC DE LA ROCHEFOUCAULD (1613–80)
Maxims

The seductive woman is the demon who makes men enter hell through the gates of paradise.

ANONYMOUS

Women are at ease in perfidy, as are serpents in bushes.

OCTAVE FEUILLET (1821–1890)

Men say of women what pleases them; women do with men what pleases them.
SOPHIE SEGUR (1799–1874)
Les Mémoires d'un Âne

Women are rakes by nature and prudes by necessity.
DUC DE LA ROCHEFOUCAULD (1613–80)
Maxims

Few women need to be loved; most of them only want to be preferred.
MLLE CLAIRE DE LESPENASSE (1732–1776)
Letters

A coquette is a woman who places her honour in a lottery; ninety-nine chances to one that she will lose it.
ANONYMOUS

I'd rather be known as a happy whore than as a chaste and desperate wife.
PIETRO ARETINO (1492–1556)
Conversations

Our husbands never appreciate anything in us. We have to go to others for that.
OSCAR WILDE (1854–1900)
Complete Works

Most women caress sin before embracing penitence.
ANONYMOUS

If you see a handsome man, act while your
    passion's hot,
Speak your mind, seize him by his parts, and
    above all do not,

Tell him, 'I'd like to be your brother and
    I admire you'
Or modesty will shut the door to what you
    want to do.
    ADAIOS

Don't keep a man quessing too long – he's sure
to find the answer somewhere else.
    MAE WEST (1892–1984)
    Goodness Had Nothing To Do With It

Women's thoughts are ever turned upon
appearing amiable to the other sex. They talk
and move and smile with a design upon us,
every feature of their faces, every part of their
dress, is filled with snares and allurements.

There would be no such animals as prudes or coquettes in the world were there no such animal as man.
JOSEPH ADDISON (1672–1719)
Essays

A woman who has made advances never remembers them without rage, unless she has reason to remember them with pleasure.
THE DICTIONARY OF LOVE (1924)

She who trifles with all is less likely to fall
Than she who but trifles with one.
JOHN GAY (1685–1732)
Fables

An amorous maiden antique
Locked a man in her house for a week;
    He entered her door
    With a shout and a roar
But his exit was marked by a squeak.
ANONYMOUS

Sometimes your lover to incite the more,
Pretend your husband's spies beset the door:
Though free as Thais, still affect a fright,
For seeming danger heightens the delight.
OVID (43 BC–AD 18)
Ars Amatoria

An immodest young woman is someone who would look better covered up.
JEAN HARLOW

THE CURIOUS WANTON.

Miss Chloe in a wanton way.
Her durgling would needs survey.
Before the glass displays her thighs
And at the sight with wonder cries.
Is this the thing that day and night
Make men fall out and madly fight
The source of sorrow and of Joy.
Which king and beggar both employ.
How grim it looks yet enter in
You'll find a fund of sweets begin.

The Devil, having nothing better to do,
Went off to tempt my lady Poltagrue.
My Lady, tempted by a private whim,
To his extreme annoyance, tempted him.
> HILAIRE BELLOC (1870–1953)
> *On Lady Poltagrue, a Public Peril*

Having already bathed, her toilet was simple. Stripping, she sprayed her body with a dainty, love-provoking perfume, rouged her lips and coloured her cheeks. Satisfied that no-one else was about, she slipped into a loose-fitting black, lacy dress and prepared her seductive trap.
> THE CONFESSIONS OF LADY BEATRICE (1899)

She uttered a quivering cry. 'Now you are much more like an eagle, waiting to strike. Why don't you, I wonder and – and take what you want?'
> ETHEL M. DELL (1881–1939)
> *The Way of an Eagle*

A wanton young lady of Wimley,
Reproached for not acting more primly,
    Answered, 'Heavens above!
    I know sex isn't love,
But it's such an attractive facsimile.'
> ANONYMOUS

But where is the woman, if she is very much in love, who will think of demanding of her lover to respect her, at that moment when love has absorbed every faculty of reason, at that moment when all life is concentrated in the fulfilment of an all-devouring desire? She is not to be found.
> GIOCOMO CASANOVA (1725–98)
> *Mémoires*

She blushed to see her innocence betrayed
And the small opposition she had made;
Yet hugg'd me close and with a sigh did say,
Once more, my dear, once more, etcetera.
JOHN WILMOT, SECOND EARL OF ROCHESTER
(1647–80)
Etcetera, A Song

Now is she in the very lists of love,
Her champion mounted for the hot
    encounter:
All is imaginary she doth prove,
He will not manage her, although he mount
    her.
WILLIAM SHAKESPEARE (1564–1616)
Venus and Adonis

When a woman's lips say, 'It is enough,' she looks at you with her eyes and they say, 'Again'.
JEAN CHAMPION

A dame that knows the ropes isn't likely to get tied up.
MAE WEST (1892–1984)
Goodness Had Nothing To Do With It

Nay, how few matches would go forward if the hasty lover did but know how many little tricks of lust and wantoness his coy and seemingly bashful mistress had oft before been guilty of?
ERASMUS (*c*. 1467–1536)
In Praise of Folly

This woman was having an affair. She used to have sex with one man in the afternoon and then she'd go back to her boyfriend and have sex with him in the evening. She'd be extra good in the evenings; she was extra guilty.
    WILLIAM LEITH
    Independent on Sunday

Show me but one who, tho' inconstant as
The rising winds or flowing seas, still
Swears not fealty to the reigning object,
Nay, fancies he shall surely keep it, too,
Tho' he has broke ten thousand vows before.
    MARY DELARIVIÈRE MANLEY (1663–1724)
    The Royal Mischief

A woman was once asked by a man why, if the pleasure of intercourse was equal for both sexes, it was generally the man who pursued and seduced the woman rather than vice versa. She replied, 'It is a very wise custom that compels men to take the initiative. For it is certain that we women are always ready for sex. That is not true for you men and we would be soliciting men in vain if they should happen not to be in the proper condition for it.'
    BRACCIOLINI POGGIO (1380–1459)
    Facetiae

Some people are so self-centred that even in love they manage to be preoccupied with their own passion to the exclusion of their lover.
    DUC DE LA ROCHEFOUCAULD (1613–80)
    Maxims

With women as with warriors, there's no robbery – all's conquest.

DOUGLAS JERROLD (1803–57)
The Story of a Feather

Pleased with the sweet Defeat, she clings
    more close,
And hugs the Conqueror that gives the
    murthering blows.

MAXIMIANUS ETRUSCUS

From the poetry of Lord Byron they drew a system of ethics compounded of misanthropy and voluptuousness, a system in which the two great commandments were to hate your neighbour and to love your neighbour's wife.

THOMAS MACAULAY (1800–59)
Essays

Love your neighbour – and if he happens to be tall, debonair and handsome, it will be that much easier.

MAE WEST (1892–1984)
Goodness Had Nothing To Do With It

A man always pats himself on the back when he has composed a letter that breathes devotion but would not be negotiable in a breach of promise suit.

HENRY ROWLAND (1871–1936)
Miscellany

Jealousy will often disclose what a thousand wiles have hid.

ALAIN GONONEZ

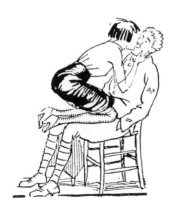

If any secret acts should be discovered,
deny them black, though they are clear as
  day.
Neither be meek nor warmer than your
  custom,
meekness and warmth are often signs of
  guilt.
OVID (43 BC–AD 18)
Ars Amatoria

Virtue, with some women, is but the precaution
of locking doors.
PETER LEMONTEY

'Will you open this door,' he heard her say. 'I
know very well she's in there with you.' And
immediately like those libertines who're turned
on by the fear of being caught in the act, out in
the open, on the river bank, or on a park bench,
he recovered his powers and while the voice
continued to row outside the room he experienced immense enjoyment in the hurry and
panic of a man running at risk, interrupted and
rushed in the midst of his lust.
JORIS-KARL HUYSMANS (1848–1907)
A. Rebours

To 'Get out of my house!' and 'What do you want
with my wife?' there is no answer.
MIGUEL CERVANTES (1547–1616)
Don Quixote

One man's folly is another man's wife.
ANONYMOUS

A lover has all the virtues and all the defects
that a husband has not.
    HONORÉ DE BALZAC (1799–1850)
    Comédie Humaine

A man firmly believes that if he can only keep
his wife on the straight and narrow path, he
can go out and zig-zag all over the downward
one without falling from grace.
    HENRY ROWLAND (1871–1936)
    Miscellany

Pray do tell me of my crime
For I'd never do to fine ladies
What I wouldn't do with my wife.
    ANONYMOUS
    The Blameless Lecher (c.1804)

Wives are young men's mistresses, companions
for middle age, and old men's nurses.
    FRANCIS BACON (1561–1626)
    Apophthegms

Funny how a married man who is trying to seduce you always begins by telling you what a trying disposition his wife has.
    HENRY ROWLAND (1871–1936)
    Miscellany

He's a fool that marries, but he's a greater that does not marry a fool. What is wit in a good wife for but to make a man a cuckold?
    WILLIAM WYCHERLEY (1641–1715)
    The Country Wife

Lament him, Mauchlins husbands a',
He often did assist ye;
For had ye staid whole weeks awa',
Your wives they ne'er had missed ye.
    ROBERT BURNS (1759–96)
    Lament Him!

Why droops my Celia?
Thou hast in place of a base husband found
A worthy lover; use thy fortune well,
With secrecy and pleasure.
    BEN JONSON (1572/3–1637)
    Volpone

Ask all the young fellows of the town if they do not lose more time, like huntsman, in starting the game than in running it down. One knows not where to find 'em, who will or will not.
    WILLIAM WYCHERLEY (1641–1715)
    The Country Wife

A clever, ugly man every now and then is successful with the ladies, but a handsome fool is irresistible.

WILLIAM MAKEPEACE THACKERAY (1811–63)
Vanity Fair

A man's ideal woman is the one he couldn't get.

ANONYMOUS

No lover should be deprived of his privileges except for an excellent reason.

DE L'AMOUR

Men lose more conquests by their own awkwardness than by any virtue in the woman.

NINON DE LENCLOS (1620–1705)
Memoires

It is my advice that in all your amours you should prefer older women to young ones. Having made a young girl miserable may give you frequent bitter reflection; none of which can attend the making of an old woman happy. They are so grateful.

BENJAMIN FRANKLIN (1706–90)
Poor Richard's Almanac

What about guilt, compunction and such stuff?
I've had my fill of all that cock;
It'll wear off, as usual.

KINGSLEY AMIS (1922–)
Nothing to Fear

Next to the pleasure of making a new mistress is that of being rid of an old one.
    WILLIAM WYCHERLEY (1641–1715)
    The Country Wife

I will not say in what particular year of his life the Duke of Argyle succeeded with me. Ladies scorn dates! Dates make ladies nervous and stories dry.
    HARRIETTE WILSON (1786–1846)
    Memoirs

Afterwards she spoke to me most disobligingly, telling me that I was one of those little womanisers who were the scourge of her sex, but that all those she met she punished likewise.
    NICOLAS RESTIF DE LA BRETONNE (1734–1806)
    Monsieur Nicolas

At last, by a supreme effort, she snatched herself from his arms, and with her dress still open, disappeared into the little garden, hearing from the outside the young master-at-arms cry out upon the threshold in anger and astonishment, 'What a strange lady! Madam desires, and then, and then Madam does not!'
    EDMOND DE GONCOURT (1822–96)
    La Faustin

A more voluptous night I never enjoyed. Five times I was fairly lost in supreme rapture. She was madly fond of me; she declared I was a prodigy and asked me if this was not extraordinary for human nature. I said twice as

much might be, but this was not, although in my own mind I was somewhat proud of my performance.

JAMES BOSWELL (1740–95)
Life of Samuel Johnson

Oh, we made the bad world go away for a minute, that really is what love is for, but when it comes back, we have of course to live in it.

MALCOLM BRADBURY (1932–)
Rates of Exchange

It is not safe to praise to a friend the object of your success; so soon as he believes your praises, he slips into your place.

OVID (43 BC–AD 18)
Ars Amatoria

No man can understand why a woman should prefer a good reputation to a good time.

HENRY ROWLAND (1871–1936)
Miscellany

It is better to love two too many than one too few.

SIR JOHN HARINGTON (*c.* 1561–1612)
Epigrams

Your women of honour, as you call them, are only chary of their reputations, not their bodies. 'Tis scandal they would avoid, not men.

WILLIAM WYCHERLEY (1641–1715)
The Country Wife

This shows Love's chiefest magic lies
In women's cunts, not in their eyes:
There Cupid does his revels keep,
There lovers all their sorrows steep;
For having once but tasted that,
Their mysteries are quite forgot.
SIR GEORGE ETHEREGE (?1634–91)
She Would if She Could

Was ever Mortal Man like me,
Continually in Jeopardy,
And always, silly Prick, by thee!
JOHN WILMOT, SECOND EARL OF ROCHESTER
(1647–80)
Sodom

A woman is never displeased if we please
several other women, provided she is preferred.
It is so many more triumphs for her.
NINON DE LENCLOS (1620–1705)
Memoires

A man may seduce every day and every hour of
the day and he is never reproached – there is no
such thing as a fallen man, only a fallen woman
or a girl.
W.N. WILLIS

She hugged the offender, and forgave the
offence:
Sex to the last.
JOHN DRYDEN (1631–1700)
All for Love

The seducer's pardoned but the husband punished.

ANONYMOUS

Faces may change, but fanny is but fanny still,
And he that screws is slave to woman's will.

JOHN WILMOT, SECOND EARL OF ROCHESTER
(1647–80)
Sodom

While alone to myself I repeat all her charms,
She I loved may be locked in another man's
    arms,
She may laugh at my cares, and so false she
    may be,
To say all the kind things she before said to
    me!
Oh then 'tis, oh then, I think there's no Hell
Like loving too well.

CHARLES II (1630–85)
Loving Too Well

A wise lover, like a good cook, is one who knows when the fire is out.

ANONYMOUS

Confucius say: 'Difficult to finish with woman who was easy to begin.'

THE RIBALD CONFUCIUS

May I grow languid in the work of Venus,
when I die, may I perish in the act;
And may a friend, weeping over my body,
say this of me: 'He died as he had lived'.

OVID (43 BC–AD 18)
Ars Amatoria